To the one and only
Callista Gingrich .
Thank you for
all your help.
Your friend
[signature]

D1315835

Dear Callista
I am so grateful for
your enthusiasm and
encouragement of this
book. Wishing you all
the best!
Ad Astra,
[signature]

Let's Chat About

Economics!

basic principles through everyday scenarios

Michelle A. Balconi & Dr. Arthur Laffer

Illustrations by Mary A. Kinsora

GICHIGAMI PRESS

With love and gratitude to my husband and children
- our chats lead to fun adventures! -mb

Table of Contents

Introduction

Chapter 1: Grocery Store   1

Chapter 2: Family Trip   9

Chapter 3: Summertime   17

Chapter 4: Yard Sale   25

Glossary of Terms   34

About the Authors & Illustrator   36

Introduction

Choices. Every day, people decide which shirt to wear, which TV show to watch or what to eat for lunch. When a choice is made it shows that something was more important than the options not chosen. Which would you prefer - a peanut butter and jelly sandwich or a vegetable and cheese wrap? There is no right or wrong answer, but you believe one will make you happier.

The world around us is created by the choices people make and can be the subject of fun conversations with children. Have you ever discussed with your child why a pair of sneakers marked with a professional athlete's name costs more than plain white canvas sneakers? It's a great time to chat about **economics**!

Economics is the scientific study of the choices people make to be happy considering they can't have everything they **need** or **want** at once. In a world of **scarce** resources, **supply** refers to things that are available and **demand** describes how many people want those things. The **price** of something you want to buy is not randomly selected but is determined as a result of supply and demand. If you choose the peanut butter and jelly sandwich for lunch, the veggie wrap becomes the **opportunity cost**, the thing you did not choose. Eating two lunches could be too much, an example of **diminishing returns**, when the cost outweighs the benefit. That's just how easy it is to chat with the children in your life about economics.

Talking about economics with children can be as familiar as discussing lunch choices or how they spend their time. Using real economic terms and pointing out the principles in everyday life, expands children's knowledge and empowers them to make choices that serve them.

Reading and chatting about economics teaches children to see themselves as a unique and scarce resource that has significant **<u>value</u>**. When adults and children discuss the economic principles together a connection is formed to explain how decisions are made. Best of all, adults provide children with a strong foundation of how the world works resulting in rich critical thinking and conversation.

Economics is an important factor in shaping the world around us, yet many adults do not feel comfortable enough with the subject to explain and point out examples to children. We've written this book to facilitate a conversation between adults and children and to illustrate how economics is a part of our daily lives. Each chapter provides familiar examples and we hope these stories will lead to ongoing discussions within your family. Terms that are **<u>bold and underlined</u>** are listed in a glossary at the back of this book for reference and better understanding.

Just because economics is taught at the highest levels of academia doesn't mean it is only useful to adults. Children can understand and apply this common-sense approach to decision-making with most opportunities in life. So whether you are discussing lunch, how to spend your time after school or even why the newest electronic gadget costs so much, sharing the basic economic principles empowers children to make well-informed choices for their own happiness.

Now, let's chat about economics!

Chapter 1
Grocery Store

Jack's family was planning a special dinner because his grandparents were coming to visit. Grandma and Grandpa lived a few hours away and would stay in the family's apartment for the weekend. Mom planned to make turkey, mashed potatoes, gravy, green beans, a salad and cornbread.

It was springtime, not Thanksgiving, and they planned this meal because it was a family favorite. Jack's younger sister Katie was especially excited about an apple pie for dessert because it was Grandpa's request and she was in charge of baking it.

The factory where Dad worked for several years recently closed and he was looking for a new job. Until he was working again, Dad and Mom explained to the kids that they needed to be more watchful about how they spent their money and use careful planning.

Dad asked Jack to bring the bag of returnable cans with him to the store so they could use the deposits to help buy groceries. While Mom and Katie cleared the kitchen table, Dad and Jack set out for the grocery store with a list of ingredients.

Clunk, clunk, clunk … Dad and Jack took turns loading the cans into the returnable machines.

"Wow, I didn't know we had so many cans to return," said Jack.

"It adds up quickly," said Dad. "It looks like we have just more than $3 to subtract from our total grocery bill at the checkout counter."

"Is it like a coupon?" asked Jack.

"Not exactly. We are getting money back for the cans because it was part of the **price** we paid when we bought them. It's called a deposit," explained Dad.

Jack nodded and walked around the corner to pick out a grocery cart. As he headed toward the center aisle he noticed there were far fewer turkeys for sale than there were last November when he came with Mom.

"Where are all of the big cases of frozen turkeys that used to be here?" wondered Jack.

Dad explained that the store carried a lot more turkeys several months ago in November because customers liked to buy them for Thanksgiving.

"When we want to buy something but the amount to choose from is limited, that's called **scarcity**. Most people want to cook a turkey for Thanksgiving, so the store has to carry a lot more that time of year to keep up with the **demand**," Dad explained.

"What's demand?" asked Jack.

"Demand is how we measure the amount of something people want to buy," said Dad. "Right now, turkey farmers and grocers know that not as many people want to cook turkey dinners, so the **supply** of turkeys is lower now but will be higher in November. Farmers who raise turkeys hatch more eggs in July and August to plan for more people buying the birds in November."

"I get it," said Jack. "There are not as many turkeys for sale now, but there are a lot of hams available because Easter is just a few weeks away."

"Exactly, the supply of turkeys is lower now, but the store will carry a lot more just before Thanksgiving time again," said Dad.

Dad loaded a medium-sized turkey into Jack's cart and started walking toward the flower section of the store.

"Supply and demand affects the price of things we want to buy, too," said Dad as he selected a bouquet of flowers for the dinner table. "That's why I can buy red roses

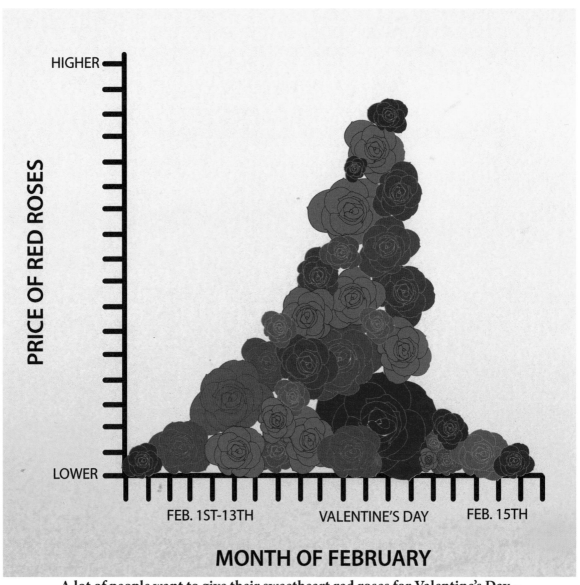

HIGHER

PRICE OF RED ROSES

LOWER

FEB. 1ST-13TH   VALENTINE'S DAY   FEB. 15TH

MONTH OF FEBRUARY

**A lot of people want to give their sweetheart red roses for Valentine's Day –
as demand increases, so does price!**

for Mom now at a cheaper price than on Valentine's Day."

"Everyone wants red roses on Valentine's Day!" blurted Jack.

"Yes, when demand increases for a scarce resource, such as red roses, so does price," explained Dad. "Red roses are an example of something we **want**, but don't **need**."

Jack quickly raced the grocery cart around a corner, and Dad shouted, "Look out!"

4

Jillian, a college student and the family's babysitter, jumped up to dodge the speeding cart.

"Oops," said Jillian. "I'll be out of your way in a minute. I'm just making some price changes."

Jillian explained that the store manager asked her to mark down the green shamrock sugar cookies that were left over from St. Patrick's Day.

Jack grinned widely and asked Dad if they could buy a box of cookies that were originally $3.99 but now were only $1.99.

"Sure, Jack, I guess eating cookies that were baked a few days ago is a pretty good deal for under $2," said Dad. "Maybe we should buy a second batch for Katie's soccer team practice. The store will sell out quickly at this lower price."

"It makes me wish Mom didn't buy them last week at $3.99," said Jack. "I guess the demand was higher before St. Patrick's Day than it is now."

"You are right, Jack. Prices are higher when demand is high and the supply is limited, but the price is lower when not as many people want to buy," explained Dad.

That all seemed to make sense to Jack. It reminded him of the high price of that new video game he wanted for Christmas, but then it went on sale a few months later.

They continued shopping for the items on Mom's list. Potatoes – check, two pounds of green beans – check, veggies for the salad – check. All that was left on Mom's list were the apples for Grandpa's pie.

Jack picked his favorite apples out of the bin, counting by twos because Mom said Katie would need eight for the pie.

"Two, four, six …," counted Jack.

"Hold on, buddy! We can buy a dozen apples in a bag for a lower price than we can by picking out eight, individually," said Dad.

"What difference does it make?" asked Jack.

"Well, the bag has a few more apples than we need, but the price per apple is a little less. We can put the apples Katie doesn't use for the pie in the fruit basket and dip them in peanut butter or caramel for snacks."

"But how are we getting more apples but paying less?" asked Jack.

Dad explained that the store gets a cheaper price on the bagged apples than the ones that are individually shipped. Different types of apples have their own unique tastes, some sweet, some sour, and good-tasting popular apples cost slightly more to buy because they are in higher demand. Since Katie was baking a pie and adding sugar to the apple filling, they could buy the cheaper apples for the recipe.

"That's right," said a voice from down the aisle. It was Mr. Martin, the store manager and Jack's little league baseball coach. "More customers prefer to buy bags of apples, so I order them in a higher quantity to get a cheaper price. Because I get a lower price, I can pass that savings along to customers while still covering my **costs**," said Mr. Martin.

"Costs?" asked Jack. "Is that how much you pay the farmer for the apples?"

"Yes," said Mr. Martin. "Plus all of the costs to run the store. We pay rent for the building, electricity for the lights and refrigerators, hourly **wages** for the store employees, and also **taxes**. Taxes pay for local schoolteachers, police officers and fire fighters."

 "Mr. Martin pays the costs of the food he sells, the people and services to run the store, sets the price of the groceries, all while thinking about the supply and demand of what he is selling," explained Dad.

After they redeemed the credit from the returnable cans and paid for their groceries, Jack and Dad wheeled the cart out to the parking lot and loaded the bags into the back of the car.

Beep, beep, beep. Jack turned to watch a large delivery truck back up to a side door of the grocery store. A worker then rolled out a metal ramp and pushed crates of milk into the building.

"I guess milk is something people want to buy all of the time. I know Mom wants Katie and me to drink it all of the time!" scowled Jack as he rolled his eyes.

"You got it. Milk is always in demand," Dad said as he patted Jack on the back. "With just a quick trip to the grocery store, you've learned how a **market economy** works. Products and services are priced according to how many of those things are available and how many people want to buy them. Now let's get these groceries home so the family feast can begin!"

Chapter 2
Family Trip

Maria stared through the kitchen window at the falling snow as she slowly placed one piece of popcorn at a time in her mouth. She usually loved watching the soft flakes gently land on the grass in her backyard, but this time it made her grumpy.

"Ugh, I wish we were going on a tropical vacation like the Golden family," moaned Maria. "I just want to paint my toenails and run around barefoot instead of wearing thick socks and boots all of the time. Is that too much to ask?!"

Mom set down her dish towel, turned and leaned against the kitchen counter. "It sounds like someone has a case of cabin fever," she said.

"I just don't understand why we can't fly to Florida or California for spring break in two weeks," said Maria.

"How about if we enjoy the extra-long winter weather we are having this year and go skiing and sledding nearby instead? I was planning to ask for a few days off from work so we can visit the art museum, go bowling and maybe take Dad to lunch at that new deli near his office," suggested Mom.

"That sounds exactly like our winter break," yawned Maria. "Don't you want to go swimming … feel the sand between your toes … and just run around outside, Mom?"

"Honey, yes I do, but it's expensive to buy airline tickets, rent a car and pay for a hotel room for the week," replied Mom.

"What's all the noise about?" sneered Danny as he walked by and grabbed the bowl of popcorn from his sister.

"Mom won't let us go on a trip for spring break," pouted Maria as she took back the popcorn bowl.

"Listen kids, if you really want to go on a trip, then find a way. Work out a plan to enjoy the warmest temperature for the least amount of expense," sighed Mom as she went back to drying the dishes.

"Us?" asked Danny. "Why do WE have to figure it out?"

"Wait, this is great! Mom just said we can plan the whole trip ourselves! Let's fly to a tropical island and go cliff diving!" squealed Maria. "I bet we can even swim with dolphins!"

Both kids jumped up and gave each other high fives. Maria ran out of the room.

"Where are you going?" asked Mom.

"To find my suitcase and my bathing suit," said Maria.

"Not so fast," said Mom. "Your plan sounds expensive and I'm not sure I can take that much time off from work. How much are the airplane tickets? What about the hotel, meals and other **costs**?"

"Oh," said Danny. "Mom said the warmest temperature for the least expense."

"Oh," said Maria. "I forgot that part."

"Maybe you two should do some research before you drag out your suitcases," Mom said and winked. "This is a great time for you to learn about **trade-offs** anyway."

"I don't want to learn. I want to swim!" said Maria.

Mom laughed. "There's nothing wrong with wanting to swim, just make a **choice** and consider the costs involved and whether it is worth it. Trade-offs are when you give up one thing in favor of something else."

"Do you mean like when I choose between having a waffle or an omelette after church?" asked Maria.

"Yes or whether you should study for a test or hang out with friends. Now all you have to do is use that same kind of decision-making to plan a trip," said Mom.

"Come on, I've got an idea!" said Danny.

Maria followed Danny and sat next to him as he turned on the computer. "There are always cheap airline tickets on the Internet. I've seen the TV commercials," whispered Danny.

They searched and searched but found only a few tickets that would take them to tropical locations. The flights that were still available departed at 5 a.m., had several stops and landed after midnight. Those flights would take up a whole day of their time off from school and the price per ticket was very high.

"Grrrr," said Maria. "Mom and Dad will never go for that, plus there are probably no hotel rooms left either."

"You are right about that," said Mom, unexpectedly calling out from the next room.

"What if we drove to Florida, like some other families are doing?" suggested Danny.

"I don't know. How far is it?" asked Maria.

A quick search revealed 18 hours of driving would get them to the closest Florida beaches.

"Hmmmm," said Danny. "Mom and Dad can split the driving. It wouldn't be that bad."

"But I heard Dad say he has a work project due by the end of the month and that he can't take any time off," said Maria.

"You are also right about that," said Mom, her eavesdropping was amusing to her but not to the children. "Paying for the gas would be much less than the airline tickets, but that is way too much driving for me to do by myself, at least in one day."

"OK," said Danny. "Flying anywhere is out, driving 18 hours is too much for Mom and would be kind of boring for us. I guess we are staying here for spring break."

"Grrrr," said Maria again as she squinted through the now snow-covered window. "Trade-offs …"

"Right," said Danny. "Trade-offs … in this case, we really want to go somewhere warm and far away but we are choosing to stay at home because of the time and expense."

"What if we still went some place warm, or at least warmer than here, but it was not too far away?" asked Maria.

Maria and Danny plan a trip with the warmest temperature for the least expense.

"Now you understand **<u>diminishing returns</u>**," Mom said smartly as she entered the room. "You've figured out that a benefit of something, like a tropical vacation, is not as great when the costs increase. In this case, the time and money of a tropical vacation are pretty high costs. At some point, the cost or effort of something increases so much that it outweighs the benefit or fun you think you will have."

"So," said Maria, "you are saying we could drive to sunny Florida but it would take two of our vacation days to get there and two back. That is four days of driving and leaves only two or three days of fun."

"Yes," said Mom. "Four days in the car is the trade-off for three days at the beach. Is it worth it to us?"

"I'd say anything that is more than a day of driving is an example of diminishing returns," pointed out Danny.

"I'd say the same," said Mom as she headed back into the kitchen. "And I'm the one actually doing the driving."

Maria sighed, "I just want to paint my toenails purple with blue dots and swim outside."

"Okay, so what temperature do we need to swim outside?" asked Danny.

"That's exactly what I was thinking! How about mid-70s," offered Maria.

Within a few minutes, they were staring at a colorful map illustrating average temperatures for the month. Lots of cities south of them had desirable forecasts, most were located about halfway between home and the Florida beaches. Surely Mom would agree to drive for a day so they could warm up 40 degrees.

"Mom!" the kids shouted together.

"Yes?" inquired Mom with raised eyebrows and a smirk on her face.

"If we drive about 9 hours south, we can swim in temperatures averaging 76 degrees," said Danny. "But a second day of driving is too much to only warm up ten more degrees."

"Oh, but what about cliff diving and swimming with dolphins and putting our toes in the sand?" asked Mom. "Sounds like those fun activities are now **opportunity costs**."

"Huh?" said Maria as she wrinkled her nose.

"You are now suggesting a closer destination and activities in a milder climate so the tropical vacation and all that goes along with it are the opportunity costs of making that choice. The option you did not choose becomes the cost of the thing you did choose," explained Mom.

"I can think of a lot of examples of opportunity costs," said Danny as he frowned. "Like when I competed in the swim meet instead of going to the concert with my friends. Or, when I ran in the 5K race for the animal shelter fund-raiser instead of going to Bobby's birthday party. The opportunity cost was having fun with my friends."

"Yes, but you decided that supporting your swim team and your community were slightly more important to you on those days," reminded Mom. "Another example of opportunity cost would be when you chose to play video games instead of studying for your math test last week and then got a low score. You chose extra time playing video games, but not earning a higher grade was the price you paid."

"Oh, I forgot about that," said Danny.

"I guess the tropical vacation is not as important now that we think about it," said Maria. "Instead, we can swim in a pool and play basketball and tennis, and I can still paint my toenails and go barefoot outside!"

"Is that what this is really about?" asked Danny. "Painting your toenails and going barefoot?"

"YES!" exclaimed Maria.

Chapter 3
Summertime

Brrrrring!! Hundreds of kids ran screaming down the steps and out to the back field as the bell finally rang at Lincoln Junior High School. They were free for the summer and didn't care that it was blistering hot outside.

Andrew and his friend Jimmy walked home from school and talked about all the fun they would have during the next ten weeks.

"I'm going to sleep in, swim and go fishing every day," said Jimmy. "Then we are going to visit our cousins in Virginia and tour Washington, D.C. Did you know most of the museums are free in the capital?"

"Cool! Fishing and swimming sound good to me," said Andrew. "We are not going on any trips but I'd really like to see the Wright Brothers' airplane that we learned about in history this year. I think it is in one of the **government's** Smithsonian museums, but I didn't know I could see it for free."

"What are you doing?" asked Andrew's younger sister, Sarah, as she pulled up next to the boys on her bike.

"Talking about all the fun we are going to have this summer," said Andrew. "Too bad you are not going to have fun because I've decided to make you do all of my chores!"

"Fine with me, that just means I'll collect all of your allowance!" teased Sarah as she sped away.

"You can have it," Andrew called after her.

"Yeah, what do you need money for during the summer anyway?" asked Jimmy. "Fishing worms are free in your yard." The boys gave each other a high five and laughed.

When Andrew arrived home a few minutes later, Sarah was sitting at the kitchen table eating a snack.

"I sure am glad I'm taking over your chores this summer," Sarah said to Andrew as he walked into the house. "Mom said now is a good time to start our savings accounts so she's making us put half of everything we earn in the bank. At least I'll be collecting double the allowance so I still have the same amount of money to spend."

"Ha," said Andrew. "Now I know I made the right decision to stop getting allowance for chores. That's not even worth it. What do you need money for anyway? Mom and Dad give us food and clothes. What else do you need?" he asked.

"Jordan and I want to go to the movie matinee every Friday this summer, plus a snack shack just opened at the park," said Sarah.

"No big deal," said Andrew. "I'm sure Mom and Dad will give me some extra spending money once in a while this summer."

"Oh?" said Mom as she walked past the kitchen carrying a laundry basket full of clothes. "That's what your allowance is for, remember?"

"Mom! You can't do that!" whined Andrew. "Summer is for taking it easy and relaxing!"

"Dad and I talked about it and decided you can continue your chores for spending money but you need to also learn to save some of it for later," explained Mom. "If you decide to complete your chores every week, you'll receive allowance but half of it will go in the bank."

"That's too much to save and soooooo not worth it," complained Andrew. "I'd rather not do chores and just do free stuff all summer."

"Like what kind of free stuff?" asked Mom.

"Like go to the park every day to fish and swim. I have a fishing pole and I'll dig up the worms from the garden. And swimming, that is totally free!" exclaimed Andrew.

"Well, you are right about most of that," said Mom. "But you'll need to buy a fishing **license** and you'd better pack a lunch because you won't have spending money for the new snack shack. I hear the milk shakes are really good, too."

Mom explained to Andrew that at his age, a $5 fishing license was required once a year. The money collected by the town from selling the licenses helped pay for keeping the lake in good condition. She said a fishing license was an example of **quid pro quo** because you directly received something for the fee you paid.

Mom also explained that the town's lake park was not really free to everyone because part of the **property taxes** she and Dad paid each year for their house went toward covering the costs of the lawn services, lifeguards, bathroom maintenance and new picnic tables. **Taxes** were not an example of quid pro quo because the fees paid benefited the entire community.

"Well, maybe I'll keep my chores for one week so I can buy a fishing license," said Andrew. "Then Sarah can do them for the rest of the summer!"

"Two weeks," corrected Mom. "Because half of what you earn is going into a savings account."

"I forgot about that part. What do I need a savings account for anyway?" asked Andrew.

"How about those new basketball shoes designed by your favorite professional athlete that you and your friends have been talking about? Or even a car when you graduate from high school?" asked Mom. "Dad and I can provide the basics but those things are definitely extras."

"I thought you and Dad would buy those things for me?" asked Andrew.

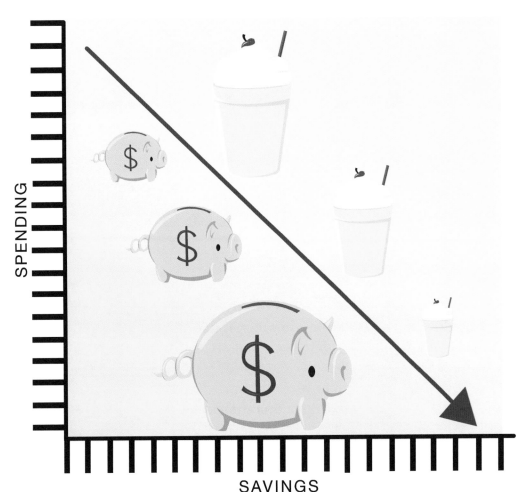

SPENDING

SAVINGS

**Andrew realizes that if he spends more on milkshakes
he will have less money to save.**

"Well, we certainly are happy to provide what you **<u>need</u>**, but those are things that you **<u>want</u>** but aren't necessary … remember nothing is free, honey," said Mom.

"That's not true! Jimmy just told me that their family is going to Washington, D.C., and all of the government museums are free!" exclaimed Andrew.

"Just because you are not paying to enter the museum doesn't mean that it is not being paid for by someone," replied Mom.

Mom explained that just as the lake park is funded by property taxes, the museums in the nation's capital are paid for by **<u>income taxes</u>** subtracted from her and Dad's paychecks. The taxes collected pay for the museum buildings, electricity, employees and artifacts.

"You keep talking about taxes. What exactly are they?" Andrew asked.

"Income tax is an amount of money taken from your paycheck that supports our town, our county, our state and our federal government to pay for public services like our military, schoolteachers and police officers and also to build highways, courthouses and even museums. There are also **sales taxes** added to the purchase price of things we buy, like backpacks for school and designer basketball shoes," Mom explained.

"Wow, that's a lot to pay for," said Andrew. "Doesn't it make you mad that you don't get to keep all of the money you make for working?"

"Well, I could decide not to work like you are choosing because we want you to save half of your allowance," said Mom. "But then we wouldn't have money for our home, food, clothes and definitely not for extras like video games. Besides, when we work and contribute to payroll, property and sales taxes that pays for important services for our community and our country."

"I get it Mom, but taking away half of everything I earn makes it not worth it to me to do my chores," said Andrew.

"I understand what you are saying and that is called a **disincentive**," explained Mom. "It happens when the cost of doing something is so high that you'd rather not do it at all. It's the opposite of **incentive**, when you are rewarded for doing something."

"That's what I've been trying to tell you," exclaimed Andrew. "Making me save half of my allowance is definitely a disincentive. I want an incentive for doing my chores."

"So earning and keeping all of your allowance gives you an incentive to do your chores," said Mom. "But that doesn't prepare you to pay for things that you will want later."

"OK," said Andrew. "How about if I save some of my allowance, but not half of it, because that is too much and makes me not want to do chores or earn allowance at all?"

"Now you are thinking. Come up with a plan for the amount of your allowance

that you are willing to save for later that will not discourage you from doing your chores and then you can talk it over with Dad and me," suggested Mom.

"Got it. I am actually excited about this now that I think about it. I mean I do want to earn money to do fun things this summer, but it is also a good idea to put some money away for later. I really can't wait for those new shoes to come out and they cost twice as much as the ones you bought me last year. I would love to have my own car when I graduate, too!"

"I'm so glad you understand the importance of saving, but I know Sarah will be very disappointed that she won't be earning your part of the allowance," remarked Mom.

"I can't wait to tell her she's not getting my allowance," smirked Andrew. "And I can't wait to tell Jimmy the museums aren't really free!"

"Now that we know nothing is really free, how about if you start earning your allowance to pay for that fishing license," said Mom as she handed the laundry basket of unfolded clothes to Andrew.

"No problem, I will," said Andrew. "Plus, I can almost taste the chocolate milk shake!"

Chapter 4
Yard Sale

Allie carefully drew a bold red diagonal line through the date on the calendar, just as she'd done for 12 squares before on as many different days.

"Eighteen days until I get my very own ePie player and I can't wait!" Allie shouted to no one in particular as she skipped out of the kitchen.

"Has she figured out how she's paying for that new gadget yet?" Dad asked Mom as they sipped coffee and read the newspaper at the kitchen table.

"You mean Allie didn't ask you? She told me she had it all worked out so I thought you agreed to pay for it," said Mom.

"I haven't heard a word about it, other than Allie marking off the days on the calendar," said Dad. He called out for Allie to join them. Allie quickly came back around the corner, sliding in her sock feet and bumping the table, spilling Dad's coffee.

"What's up?" asked Allie.

"Every day we watch you mark off another date on the calendar because you are excited about some new technology thing coming out," said Dad. "But we haven't heard how much it **costs** and how you are paying for it."

"Oh, yes, I've got it all planned out. It costs $80 and with you and Mom paying for half of it, I can come up with the rest," said Allie.

"What? $80??" gasped Dad. "For a toy?"

"Dad, it's not a toy. It's the special-edition ePie music player that comes preloaded with the new Cricket Boys' album and even has their picture on the case!" shrieked Allie. "Buying it is the only way you can hear the group's new music until it is released a month later!"

"Now I've heard everything! Why don't you just wait and listen to the radio, instead?!" exclaimed Dad. "And if you think we are paying for any part of this, you are mistaken."

"But Dad, I really, really, really need this! All of my friends are getting it!" wailed Allie. "Why can't you and Mom pay half? I thought that would be a good plan."

"We have other things to spend money on, like back-to-school supplies next month and we've just been discussing whether it's time to replace our old car," explained Dad. "Why didn't you come to us and ask instead of assuming we'd give you $40 for something you **want** and don't really **need**?"

"Dad is right. We are not paying half, so what is your plan to earn the money in less than three weeks?" asked Mom. "Or maybe now that you are paying for it yourself you realize that you don't need the ePie after all?"

"Oh, I have to buy the Cricket Boys ePie player," moaned Allie. "I just can't believe you are not willing to pay for half of it! Everyone else's parents are paying for the whole thing."

"I doubt that," said Dad.

"It's true!" exclaimed Allie.

"Well, we are not everyone else's parents. If you really want the ePie player I guess you'll have to earn the money. Isn't there another way to get it at a lower **price**?" asked Mom. "Maybe it will go on sale in a month or two."

"No," said Allie. "It's only available for a limited time. It's special. It has the Cricket Boys on it!"

"Oh," said Dad. "Unlike all of the choices we have to buy a car at different sizes and prices, there are no alternatives to buying the Cricket Boys ePie player. Buying a car is **elastic** but buying the ePie player is **inelastic**, the opposite. You have no other **choices** so you are willing to pay the high price."

"Huh?" asked Allie. "What does elastic have to do with it? It's a music player, not a rubber band!"

Dad explained that buying a car is elastic because there are a variety of choices at different prices and the **demand**, or number of people who want to buy, for cars

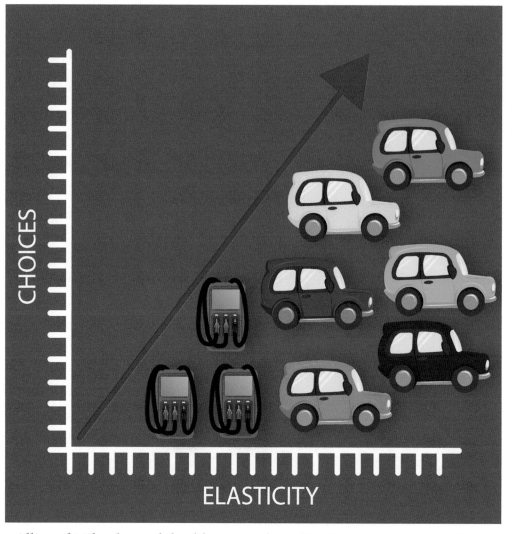

Allie and Mikey learned that like cars and gasoline the more choices you have, the more flexibility there is in price.

moves up and down like stretchy elastic as the price changes. Buying the special-edition ePie player is inelastic because even when the cost is very high, it doesn't affect the demand for it. With no other choices, people will still buy the ePie player at the high price, which means the demand is inelastic and does not move up and down.

"I guess that kind of makes sense," said Allie. "I just know I love the Cricket Boys music and really have to have this ePie player!"

"Think of it this way, Allie," started Mom. "When we buy a car, there are a lot of choices and as price changes so does the demand, making it elastic ... demand reacts to the change in price. But most cars need gas to drive and even when the price of gas becomes much higher, the demand for it remains pretty much the same, it doesn't react to a change in price. Gas is an inelastic product because about the same amount of people buy it even when the price changes."

"Even when the price is higher, I will still need gas to drive to work," said Dad.

"OK, I get it now," said Allie. "But how am I going to earn $80 in less than three weeks to pay for my inelastic Cricket Boys ePie player?"

"How were you planning to earn the money when you thought we would pay for half?" asked Mom.

"Well, the Brown family said they would pay me to babysit Scotty and Stevie," Allie said.

"Sounds great, but I don't think that will be enough in such a short time. Perhaps you should have started saving a few months ago," said Mom.

"Ugh!" said Allie. "There's got to be another way."

"I've got an idea," said Dad. "Mom and I would like to clean out the attic, basement and garage because we have a lot of things we really don't use anymore. Why don't you tackle this project and have a yard sale? You can keep the money and add it to the money you make babysitting."

"That sounds like a lot of work," said Allie.

"You can always ask your brother to help you," offered Mom, "but then you'll have to share the money with him."

"Alright," said Allie. "I better get busy!"

Allie told her brother, Mikey, about their parents' idea of holding a yard sale with things they cleaned out from the house. Mikey was really excited about the idea because he wanted to buy a skateboard he saw advertised on a sales flyer. Together, they sorted through old sports equipment, snow boots, clothes and toys. While Allie put price stickers on each item they planned to sell, Mikey made signs and posted them around the neighborhood.

On the day of the yard sale, the kids were surprised at how many of their items sold in just a few hours. Mikey and Allie were happy with the results of the yard sale and divided the earnings. Allie added it to her babysitting money from the week before and had just enough for the Cricket Boys ePie player! At the end of the day, Mom and Dad helped the kids load the remaining yard sale items into the car and took them to a donation center.

Mikey was very excited about his half of the earnings and asked Dad to take him to the store to buy a skateboard while Mom and Allie stood in line to pick up the ePie player. Mikey realized that the price he saw in the advertising flyer was for a sale that ended a few days before. While he still had just enough money to buy the skateboard including the **sales tax**, he wasn't sure he wanted to pay the higher price.

"Dad, I have enough to buy the skateboard, but look at this scooter that is half of that price. That could be fun to ride and it doesn't cost as much," said Mikey. "Or maybe I should buy this pair of rollerblades that cost more than the scooter but is still less than the skateboard."

"You have a lot of choices here," said Dad.

Allie and Mom admired Mikey's cool new rollerblades and they were surprised that he still had money left over for his piggy bank.

"I'm confused. Why did you buy rollerblades when you wanted a skateboard?" asked Allie.

"When I realized the full price of the skateboard was actually more expensive, I thought rollerblades or even a scooter would be just as much fun and they both cost less," said Mikey.

"Geez," said Allie. "I didn't have any other choices so I paid the full price for the new ePie player. It may be inelastic but the new Cricket Boys album sure sounds awesome!"

You are a unique and scarce resource with tremendous value - make choices that serve *you*!

Glossary of Terms

Choice: the decision between two or more options.

Cost: the amount of something given (money, time, effort, material, another choice) for a product or service we need or want.

Demand: the measurement of how many people need or want to have something.

Disincentive: the cost of doing something is so great that it discourages that choice.

Diminishing returns: when the cost of increasing an activity becomes greater than the benefit received from that activity.

Economics: the study of decisions people make to get things they need or want in a world of limited resources.

Elastic: the demand of something changes or reacts when the price for that product or service changes.

Government: the organized system of people that make laws controlling a country, state or other area of people.

Incentive: a reward or positive result for doing something.

Income taxes: an amount of money paid to the government from money earned by doing a job.

Inelastic: the demand of something does not change or react when the price for that product or service changes.

License: official permission from a government or authority to do some activity.

Market economy: an environment where products and services are priced according to how many of those things are available and how many people need or want to buy them.

Need: A product or service required for living.

Opportunity cost: the choice given up for the choice more strongly desired and selected.

Quid pro quo: something given for something received.

Price: the cost paid for a product or service.

Property taxes: the amount of money charged by a government for owning real estate (land and/or house).

Sales taxes: the amount of money charged by a government for the sale of products or services.

Scarce: the limited amount of anything we need or want that leads us to make choices.

Supply: the amount of products and services available.

Taxes: an amount of money charged by a government on purchases, money earned or an activity to pay for public services.

Trade-offs: giving up one thing because you prefer something else.

Value: the worth of something according to our choices.

Wages: the amount someone is paid for doing work.

Want: a product or service desired but not needed.

About the
Authors & Illustrator

Michelle Balconi is a freelance writer and speaker focused on creating connections between children and adults through economics. She loves to chat about economics because it is the only perfectly balanced science - both factual and emotional. Before writing, Michelle worked in communications for 15 years alongside technology investors introducing first-to-market products. Michelle feels fortunate to have met so many kind and interesting people as she grew up in Florida, spent many years in California and Massachusetts and now lives in Michigan with her husband and two children. When she is not writing, Michelle loves to travel and chat it up with nearly everyone she meets.

Dr. Arthur Laffer is the founder and chairman of Laffer Associates, an economic research firm focusing on interconnecting macroeconomic, political and demographic changes. Dr. Laffer was a member of President Reagan's Economic Policy Advisory Board (1981 - 1989) and was noted in *TIME* magazine's 1999 cover story as "One of the Century's Greatest Minds." Dr. Laffer is well known for the Laffer Curve, an illustration of the theory that there exists some tax rate between 0% and 100% that will result in maximum tax revenue for governments. He is a frequent cable news contributor and the author and co-author of many newspaper articles and books including *Return to Prosperity* and *An Inquiry into the Nature and Causes of the Wealth of States*. In addition to writing and speaking about economics, Dr. Laffer enjoys spending as much time as possible with his great grandchild and 11 grandchildren on their family farm where they explore nature and raise animals of many types.

Mary Kinsora Mary Kinsora is a children's book illustrator currently working out of the Detroit Metro area. Having graduated from the College for Creative Studies with a bachelor's degree in illustration, she is currently working toward the creation of a new children's media company, and her own business in licensing products from her artwork. Mary is particularly interested in stories that are imaginative but help to educate and enrich children. In her free time, Mary enjoys hiking, drinking tea, spending time with her "gang of critters," and long chats with her grandmother.

Made in the USA
Charleston, SC
28 September 2014